This book belongs to:

_____

Traveling Babies

by KATHRYN O. GALBRAITH

illustrated by JANE DIPPOLD

Traveling

NorthWord
Minnetonka, Minnesota

Babies

by Kathryn O. Galbraith

illustrated by Jane Dippold

The illustrations were created using
watercolor and colored pencil on Strathmore
The text and display type were set in Georgia and Spumoni
Art directed and designed by Lois A. Rainwater
Edited by Kristen McCurry

*The author wishes to thank Dr. Dee Boersma,
University of Washington, for generously sharing her time and expertise.*

NORTHWORD
Books for Young Readers
11571 K-Tel Drive
Minnetonka, MN 55343
www.tnkidsbooks.com

Photographs © 2006 provided by:
Bruce Coleman/Alamy: mallard ducks; Frans Lanting/Minden Pictures: emperor penguins;
Gerry Ellis/Minden Pictures: black-handed spider monkeys; Mitsuaki Iwago/Minden Pictures: red kangaroos;
Michael Quinton/Minden Pictures: common loons; Roger de la Harpe/Animals Animals-Earth Scenes: Nile crocodiles;
Adam Hart-Davis /SPL/Photo Researchers, Inc.: spiderlings; Martin Harvey/Alamy: African elephants;
Kevin Schafer/Alamy: northern sea otters; Winfried Wisniewski/FLPA/Minden Pictures: lions.

Library of Congress Cataloging-in-Publication Data

Galbraith, Kathryn Osebold.
Traveling babies / by Kathryn O. Galbraith ; illustrated by Jane Dippold.
p. cm.
ISBN 1-55971-939-7 (hardcover)
1. Animals--Infancy--Juvenile literature. I. Dippold, Jane, ill. II. Title.

QL763.G35 2006
591.3'9--dc22
2005018646

Printed in Singapore
10 9 8 7 6 5 4 3 2 1

To Steve, my favorite traveling companion.
And to Barbara, Brenda, Dave, George, Kirby and Sylvie,
dear friends and fine writers. Thank you.

—K.O.G.

For my babies, Isaac, Seth, and Bryn,
who inspire me every day.

—J.D.

Some babies scramble from place to place.

Some babies creep or crawl.

But *some* babies
travel in surprising ways.

Baby penguins...
SHUFFLE
ALONG
on papa's
broad feet.

Baby monkeys...
cling and swing
through the tops of trees.

Baby kangaroos...
bounce up and down
in a pocket of fur.

Baby loons...
hop aboard
for a
snuggle-down cruise.

Baby crocodiles...
hitch a ride
in mama's huge grin.

Baby spiders... *float and drift* on the blowing wind.

Baby mallards...
paddle, paddle, glide
in a long yellow line.

Baby elephants...
trot and sway
in the sunshine.

Baby sea otters...
sail and snooze
on mama's warm chest.

Baby lions... **bobble along** by the scruff of their necks!

And some babies travel...

Swoosh on a bike.

Beep, beep in a car.

Bump, bump in a wagon.

And slap,
slap,
slap

on two
bare feet!

Traveling Babies is KATHRYN O. GALBRAITH's twelfth book for children. She writes, "Ideas come in unexpected ways. They can also take you to unexpected places. One afternoon I noticed tiny spiderlings 'ballooning' or sailing on the wind. That one moment in the garden led me to explore the many unique and surprising ways babies move from place to place."

Ms. Galbraith lives in Tacoma, Washington, and is a frequent speaker at schools and conferences. She is also an instructor in the University of Washington's Extension Program, Writing for Children.

JANE DIPPOLD was born and raised in Ohio. She graduated from Miami University in Ohio with a degree in Fine Arts. She has illustrated many books for children, and her artwork also appears in children's magazines, on greeting cards, posters, T-shirts, calendars, and even as stuffed animals! She lives with her family in Coldwater, Ohio. See more of Jane's artwork at www.janedippold.com.